Girl Versus Squirrel

WRITTEN BY
HAYLEY BARRETT

ILLUSTRATED BY
RENÉE ANDRIANI

MARGARET FERGUSON BOOKS
HOLIDAY HOUSE · NEW YORK

Margaret Ferguson Books
Text copyright © 2020 by Hayley Barrett
Illustrations copyright © 2020 by Renée Andriani
All Rights Reserved
HOLIDAY HOUSE is registered in the U.S. Patent and Trademark Office.
Printed and bound in February 2020 at Toppan Leefung, DongGuan City, China.
www.holidayhouse.com
First Edition
1 3 5 7 9 10 8 6 4 2

Library of Congress Cataloging-in-Publication Data

Names: Barrett, Hayley, author. | Andriani, Renee, illustrator.
Title: Girl versus squirrel / Hayley Barrett ;
illustrations by Renee Andriani.
Description: First edition. | New York : Margaret Ferguson Books,
Holiday House, [2020] | Summary: "A resourceful girl named Pearl
matches wits with an intrepid squirrel in a rollicking tale of teacups, peanuts,
and the satisfying surprise of learning something new" — Provided by publisher.
Includes facts about squirrels.
Identifiers: LCCN 2019012437 | ISBN 9780823442515 (hardcover)
Subjects: | CYAC: Squirrels—Fiction. | Bird feeders—Fiction.
Classification: LCC PZ7.1.B37264 Gir 2020 | DDC [E]—dc23
LC record available at https://lccn.loc.gov/2019012437

For Rose and John, with my love—H.B.

For my parents, and those who coexist
with squirrels everywhere—R.A.

Pearl built three bird feeders.
One looked like a house.
One looked like a tube.

One looked like a teacup
perched on top of a tall pole.
It looked like a teacup
because it *was* a teacup.
Pearl was particularly proud of it.

She filled the house bird feeder with suet.

She filled the tube bird feeder with seeds.

She filled the teacup with peanuts. Lots of birds love peanuts.

Pearl took the lens caps off her binoculars and waited.

Cardinals and flickers swooped in for suet.
Finches and chickadees sailed in for seeds.
But not a single bird could settle on the teacup.
Because something else wanted those peanuts.

"Hey," protested Pearl,
"bird feeders are for birds!"
But the squirrel didn't flinch.
Instead, it flicked its tail
and gobbled Pearl's peanuts—
each and every one—before
dashing to a hole in the
old oak tree.

"Drat that squirrel!"
grumbled Pearl.
"It may be brave, but it's
no match for me.
Girl versus Squirrel
is on!"

With her hockey stick and some duct tape,
Pearl extended the teacup's pole.
"There," she said, "that's tall enough
to stop any squirrel in its tracks."

She watched, breathless with anticipated success, but was soon disappointed.

"Drat, drat that speedy squirrel," she groused. "I'll make the pole taller."

Now the teacup towered, but that didn't deter the squirrel. It scurried up the mop, scrabbled up the hockey stick, and shinnied straight up the pole.

"Oh, no," Pearl groaned. "Brave, speedy, and determined too."

The squirrel stared at Pearl and seized an especially plump peanut. But before it could take a nibble . . .

the pole began to teeter
and totter until . . .

THUD!

It toppled to the ground. The teacup popped off the pole, the handle snapped off the teacup, and the startled squirrel skedaddled to the tip-top twig of the old oak tree.

"Drat, drat, drat you, squirrel!" growled Pearl. "You're a bird-feeder-crashing, teacup-smashing, peanut-poaching pest!"

Pearl poked through grass and peanuts to find the teacup's handle and muttered, "But you will never, ever, ever be a match for me."

While Pearl glued her teacup, she pondered and plotted. Step by step, she pulled together a plan to put that squirrel to the test.

She rummaged through her box of useful odds and ends.

Then Pearl clambered and climbed,
lifted and leveled, shifted and stretched,
twisted and tied. As a network of obstacles emerged,
each more squirrel-challenging than the last,
Pearl began to enjoy herself.
"Whew," she panted.
"This is as much fun as
building bird feeders."

When everything was
ready, Pearl tumbled
more peanuts into the
teacup. "Bold, speedy, and
determined won't be enough,"
she pronounced. "This time, teacup
triumph will require nerves of
squirrely steel."

Training her binoculars on the old oak tree,
Pearl scanned up—branch by branch—until . . .

There!

"I've done my best to best you, squirrel!" shouted Pearl.
"Now let's see what you can do. Ready, set . . ."

But before she could shout GO, that squirrel was gone.
Headfirst, scuttling down the tree and . . .

Pearl was dazzled.

Then she was puzzled.

"One, two, three babies," murmured Pearl. "According to squirrel experts, the adult female tends the kits, so that must mean . . ."

The quick and nimble ninja squirrel was a mother!
Pearl's can-do, will-do, just-did squirrel . . . was quite a girl.

"I proclaim your victory," cheered Pearl, "and I salute you,
fearless, fluffy sister!"

"She'll teach them everything she knows," Pearl said. "How to climb and balance, how to think and plan. She'll develop their attention span." And then—right then—Pearl knew she wanted to help the squirrel family. And she knew how to do it.

Pearl built bird feeders.
She filled the house feeders with suet.
She filled the tube feeders with seeds.

She filled the teacups with peanuts.
Lots and lots of peanuts.

Some Squirrelly Facts

There are hundreds of squirrel species. They are native to every continent except Australia and Antarctica.

All squirrel species belong to the family *Sciuridae*. This name comes from two Greek words—*skia* and *oura*—which together mean "shadow tail."

There are three basic types: ground squirrels, tree squirrels, and flying squirrels.

Ground squirrels live in burrows. Chipmunks, marmots, and prairie dogs are all ground squirrels.

Tree squirrels often live in hollow tree cavities. They also build nests of leaves and twigs. This type of nest is called a *drey*.

Flying squirrels are also tree-dwellers. Despite their name, flying squirrels cannot truly fly. They leap and glide through the air, supported by wing-like flaps of skin called *patagia*. A new species, Humboldt's flying squirrel, was discovered in the United States in 2017.

A group of squirrels is called a *scurry*.

Squirrels are omnivorous. While they mainly eat plant-based foods like nuts, roots, and seeds, they will also consume insects, eggs, and even small animals such as baby birds.

Squirrels' front teeth never stop growing. Like all rodents, they must gnaw on wood, nutshells, and other objects to grind their teeth down.

Young squirrels are known as kits, kittens, pups, or simply as baby or infant squirrels.

Kits are born blind and are totally dependent on the mother squirrel for two or three months. Squirrels are mammals, and they drink their mother's milk until they are old enough to leave the nest. Then they'll explore the world while learning essential survival skills from the mother.

Squirrels provide the important environmental service of reseeding trees and plants. A squirrel can hide thousands of nuts each fall. The ones they don't retrieve may sprout in the spring.

In the United States, October is Squirrel Awareness Month, and National Squirrel Appreciation Day is January 21st.